LOVE SPOTS

Written by Karen Panier

Illustrated by Sabrina Brady

ISBN 978-1-61225-268-1

Published by Mirror Publishing
Milwaukee, WI 53214

Printed in the USA.

I dedicate this book to my four amazing grandchildren: Aiden, Ella, and especially Abby and Jack whose dad is a pilot in the U.S. Air Force. In addition, I want to thank my son and all military personnel who give so much of themselves while proudly wearing love spots.

Why does my uniform have so many spots?
Why? Why? Well, I will tell you why.

It's because each spot is a love spot,
so when I look at them, I think about you.

**With this spot, I think about
you swinging so high.**

A different spot, you are pretending to fly.

Point to this spot,
and I think about you watching TV.

This one makes me think about you reading a book.

That one, eating the pancakes we cook.

This spot reminds me of "Trick or Treat."

And this spot, P.U., your stinky feet.

I remember you falling and getting a bump.

I remember you pouting and being a grump.

A spot here, you are getting a bath with shampoo in your hair.

A spot there, you are going to bed after saying a prayer.

See this one? I think about you looking at bugs.

See that one? You are giving me great big hugs.

Sometimes a military mom or dad must leave for a while, and you feel sad.

Maybe I'm home
or maybe I'm not,
but I think of you
with each love spot.

I wear this uniform just for you,

so a better world will come true.

There is one more spot I must tell you about.
It's the very best spot, without a doubt.

It's always my favorite, and here's the best part,
you can find this special love spot right here,
close to my heart.

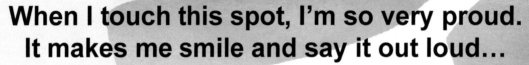

When I touch this spot, I'm so very proud.
It makes me smile and say it out loud...

My child,
I love you!

CPSIA information can be obtained
at www.ICGtesting.com
Printed in the USA
BVHW020009300122
627552BV00001B/4